ABOUT THIS BOOK

THE GOLDEN GOD: APOLLO
Doris Gates

Apollo, driver of the golden Chariot of the Sun, was the best-loved of the gods. God of medicine, protector of flocks and voyagers, he ruled in splendor from the dazzling House of the Sun. Since his birth on the floating island of Delos, his glory spread over the world—those women he loved bore him heroic sons, and those who roused his wrath found swift vengeance.

Here also are the splendid tales of:

Artemis—twin sister of Apollo and goddess of the hunt
Daphne—the lovely maiden turned into a laurel
Hermes—god of thieves
Asclepius—who raised the dead and invoked Zeus's wrath
Phaeton—Apollo's son, who dared to drive his father's chariot
Acteon—the hunter who became the prey
Orion—the great hunter who could walk on water

DORIS GATES

The Golden God
APOLLO

Illustrated by Constantinos CoConis

Puffin Books

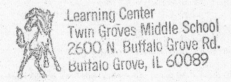

*These stories are all dedicated to
the boys and girls of
Fresno County, California,
who heard them first*

Penguin Books Ltd, Harmondsworth, Middlesex, England
Penguin Books, 40 West 23rd Street, New York, New York 10010, U.S.A.
Penguin Books Australia Ltd, Ringwood, Victoria, Australia
Penguin Books Canada Limited, 2801 John Street, Markham, Ontario, Canada L3R 1B4
Penguin Books (N.Z.) Ltd, 182–190 Wairau Road, Auckland 10, New Zealand

First published by The Viking Press 1973
Published in Puffin Books 1983
Reprinted 1986

Library of Congress Cataloging in Publication Data
Gates, Doris, date. The Golden God: Apollo.
Originally published: New York: The Viking Press, 1973.
Summary: Retells the myths surrounding the figure
of Apollo, the Greek god of medicine and music, protector
of flocks and voyagers, the most feared and best loved
of all the gods on Mount Olympus.
1. Apollo (Greek deity)—Juvenile literature.
[1. Apollo (Greek deity)   2. Mythology, Greek]
I. CoConis, Constantinos, ill.   II. Title.
BL820.A7G37 1983   292′.211   83-4002   ISBN 0-14-031647-7

Printed in the United States of America by
Offset Paperback Mfrs., Dallas, Pennsylvania

CONTENTS

The Birth
of Leto's Twins

Leto the Titan was about to give birth. She knew her offspring would be twins. Zeus had sired them, and Hera, Zeus's jealous wife, was making life unbearable for Leto. Hera threatened to destroy any spot on land or sea that dared harbor Leto during her labor. So no ruler would let her stay within his borders, and the Titan was a wanderer upon the earth as her time drew near.

At last she came to a small floating island called Delos. It could not properly be called land since it moved like flotsam on the surface of the water. Neither was it sea. As it swept near the shore on which she stood, Leto spoke to it.

"You, too, are a wanderer," she said. "I roam the

earth and you the sea. Therefore have pity on me.
Give me rest, and I promise that you will have fame
and riches."

The little island was caught by her words. Though
bright with wild flowers, it possessed no riches, not
even a grove of trees. No precious metals lay beneath
its surface, and it was too small ever to become a
mighty kingdom. Now the Titan had promised Delos
fame and riches if only she might rest within its flowery
meadows. What had Delos to fear from Hera's wrath?
It had nothing to lose!

"Very well," the island said to Leto. "Come and
rest here with me; I have little to offer but a safe birth-
place for your children."

So Leto waded to the shores of Delos, and the island
floated off with her. Very soon after that she gave birth
to twins, a boy and a girl. The boy was the god Apollo
and his sister the goddess Artemis. They were to become two of the most important of all the godly family
on high Olympus.

Poseidon the god of the sea, anchored Delos to the
ocean bottom following that birth. As the shrine of
Apollo, the golden god, the little island became fa-
mous throughout the world. Each year a festival was
held there, where a temple had been erected to Apollo
and a huge statue of the god placed before it. People
brought riches to the temple, and wealthy merchants
came to dwell there in houses worthy of the gods.
Leto's promise was abundantly fulfilled.

Apollo became the best loved of all the gods on Mount Olympus. He was the golden god, and always the brightness of sunshine surrounded him. His gifts to mankind were more precious than gold. He was god of medicine and god of music; he was associated particularly with the music of the lyre, a gift of his brother Hermes. He was the protector of flocks and of voyagers. As the god of archery, he was often feared, for his silver arrows never failed to find their mark. Apollo was often called the Far-Darter. Sometimes his arrows brought plagues upon mankind to punish man's arrogance.

He succeeded the god of the sun, Helius, the Titan, who drove the fiery chariot across the sky each day. Wearing a dazzling diadem upon his golden head, Apollo was a welcome figure to all the people of Earth, as, dispelling darkness, he brought them light and warmth.

Artemis, twin sister of Apollo, was also an archer. She was goddess of the hunt and was never without a quiver on her back and a golden bow in her hand. Her arrows sped as swiftly and as truly as those of her brother. But while Apollo's arrows brought woe to man, Artemis usually reserved hers for the hunt. The forest rang with the twang of her golden bow when she and her maidens (all of whom had taken a vow never to marry) were following the chase. Like her sister Athena, Artemis disdained romantic love. Aphrodite, goddess of love, had no power over her, and she could be cruel to any man who tried to win her favors. She was not a lovable goddess, though she often assisted women in childbirth and was the guardian of children and all young things. She avoided cities, preferring above all the shadowy depths of the forest.

Delos was helpless to protect Leto for long. Hounded by Hera, the Titan again found herself a wanderer upon the earth, now with two babies to care for. She came at last to the land of Lycia. For a long time no rain had fallen there. The sun beat fiercely down, and the fields were parched. Leto was weary, and above all, thirsty. Her children, too, were thirsty, having drained her breasts of milk. She was wondering desperately what she could do to stop their fretful crying and end her own suffering when she spied a fair-sized lake at the end of a small valley. It lay like a jewel under the hot sky, and she hastened eagerly toward it.

As she approached the water, she noticed a group of laborers gathering the reeds and osiers that grew thickly in the damp soil at the lake's edge. Carefully Leto laid her babies upon the cool ground, then knelt to drink. But hardly had she touched her lips to the water when the cruel people rushed upon her. They seized her rudely and dragged her away from the lake.

"Why are you doing this?" she cried. "I am suffering from thirst, and my children are, too. Surely the water is there for everyone. I mean you no harm by coming here only to drink. Therefore let me end my thirst."

But the people only laughed at her pleading. When she tried to fight her way back to the water, they ran before her and splashed into the lake. They kicked their feet about so that mud rose from the lake bottom, and all the water became undrinkable. Leto wept at the sight and the people taunted her.

Suddenly anger seized the Titan. She remembered she was a goddess, the beloved of Zeus. Humility fell away from her. Raising her hands to heaven she prayed, "Let these cruel people live forever in this lake."

A strange compulsion seized her tormentors as she spoke the words. They seemed unable to leave the water. Those who had crawled up onto the shore jumped back into the lake and submerged themselves. When their heads appeared above the surface, they berated Leto with voices that had become mere croakings. Suddenly their necks shortened and their heads sank down to sit directly on their shoulders. As they leaped to shore, their legs underwent a change, too. They became long and thin and supple, and webs appeared between their fingers and toes. Their bodies shrank until they were no larger than human hands. Her tormentors had been changed to frogs. Leto's prayer had been answered.

She waited until the water had cleared, then Leto and her babies drank.

The Story of Niobe

Niobe was queen in Thebes, the city founded by Cadmus. She was the proud mother of fourteen children, seven sons and seven daughters.

Leto was now a proud mother, too. Her twins were no longer children but a youth and maiden skilled in archery. Deciding the time had come for the people to do them and herself special honor, she chose the city of Thebes as the scene of this celebration. She made her wishes known to Manto, a woman who could foretell the future. Manto went through the streets calling to the women of Thebes to crown their heads and hasten to the altars.

"It is Leto herself who commands you through me," the seer told them.

The women were quick to obey her summons. They

gathered fragrant herbs and flowers and fashioned themselves crowns. Thus decorated, they hurried to the city's altars, there to burn incense and offer prayers for the Titan and her godly twins.

When news of all this reached Niobe, she was furious.

"Who is Leto that she should be honored in this way?" demanded the queen. "What has she done but give birth to two children? It would be more fitting if this feast were in my honor. I have borne fourteen handsome sons and daughters. I, too, am descended from the gods. Zeus is my grandsire, and I am as beautiful as any goddess."

Thus did Niobe scorn the Titan. Then she ordered her serving women to deck her in the very finest garment that her wardrobes held. It was a gown woven of gold thread and was as light as down. When she moved, it flowed about her slender figure, and when Niobe stood regally still, it hung in shimmering, vertical folds. Her shining hair, caught up at the sides with jeweled combs, hung down her back to blend its gold with the glistening gown. Indeed Niobe was a most beautiful woman when, surrounded by the ladies of her court, she left her palace to address the women of Thebes.

"It is absurd for you to be honoring Leto," she told them. "Take those wreaths off your heads. Leto has but two children while I can boast of fourteen. Have done with this foolish celebration."

Manto's cheeks paled as she listened to the words. She knew the danger of defying the gods, and here was the queen actually insulting one of them. No good could come of it. Yet the seer dared not go against the angry queen, though in her heart she feared for Niobe. She watched with dread as the women removed their crowns and smothered the smoldering incense.

Leto soon learned of Niobe's defiance, for the gods always knew when mortals defied or mocked them. She called Apollo and Artemis to her on the summit of Mount Cynthus, the highest point on the island of Delos. Below them were the island's heavily indented shores, the blue Aegean waters biting deep into the green land.

"The queen of Thebes has greatly insulted me," she informed the twins. "She has dared to mock me because I have only you two children while she has seven sons and seven daughters. She has even dared to destroy my altars."

Apollo broke in. "I have heard enough. The longer we stay here, the longer her punishment will be delayed."

Artemis agreed with this. Their mother watched them glide down the air toward Thebes, their bows in hand, their arrows in bronze quivers on their backs.

There was a parade ground around the walls of Thebes where the young nobles of the city liked to display their horsemanship. On well-groomed steeds bridled with gold, the sons of Niobe wheeled and galloped their chargers. The brilliance of their saddle cloths made a bright show of color against the glossy hides of the horses. One of these young princes, Tantalus, had just pulled his horse to a sudden halt when an arrow pierced his breast. He dropped his reins with a cry and slid from his saddle, dead. There was a second cry and another and another as one by one the sons of Niobe fell to the dust, pierced by the arrows of Apollo, the Far-Darter.

News of the disaster quickly reached Niobe, and she rushed from the palace, a different woman now from the proud queen who had mocked Leto such a short time before. She came stumbling, blind with grief, to bend over the bodies of her sons.

But still pride possessed her. With arms raised to heaven, she cursed Leto. "I know whom to thank for this," she cried. "Leto of the stony heart. Yet you have won no victory over me. My sons are gone and my husband for grief has taken his own life. But still I have my daughters, seven handsome maids to comfort my old age."

The daughters had followed their mother to the spot where their brothers had fallen. As Niobe finished speaking, there came the loud twang of a bow, and one of the girls dropped dead, an arrow of Artemis through her heart. Again the bow twanged, and again a daughter of Niobe fell, pierced through the breast.

When six had died, Niobe threw her body over the youngest and pleaded for her life. "Leave me this one," she prayed. "Here is my youngest, my littlest. Only leave me this one."

But even as she spoke, the girl died.

Niobe sank down among her dead. All was lost now. Her proud boasting had brought her to this.

So terrible was her grief that the gods took pity upon her and turned her into an unfeeling marble statue. But it is said that tears still run down its stone face.

Apollo
and Python

When they were grown, Apollo and Artemis were received into the family of gods on Mount Olympus. The Olympians made the occasion an important celebration. The three Graces danced, Aphrodite with them. Hebe, cupbearer of the gods, served ambrosia to Leto's twins. Once they had eaten it, they became immortal. Zeus bestowed special powers on them, and so they took their places among the family of gods.

One day, soaring through the bright sky from Delos to the mainland of Greece, Apollo came upon a mighty mountain. Below it stretched a plain lying between two mountain ranges and ending in the blue waters of a wide gulf, the gulf of Corinth. The mountain was Parnassus, and the land lying under its shadow was Delphi.

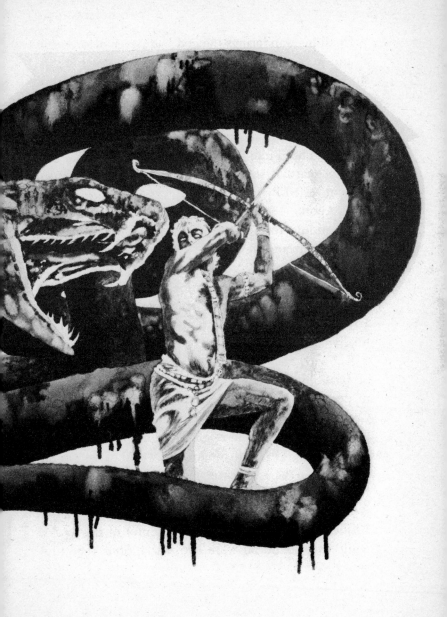

In all his wanderings the god had never before seen a land so fair. He knew at once that this must be his shrine, the seat of his oracle. For in addition to his other gifts, Apollo had the gift of prophecy. He descended to Earth, at a place where mist rose from a deep chasm. But an oracle was already established at Delphi. The Titan Themis had made it her abode, and to guard it she placed in the sanctuary a huge serpent called Python.

As Apollo was about to enter the sanctuary, Python came gliding forth, breathing fire and thrashing his great coils from side to side. The young god fitted an arrow to his bow and sent it winging into the body of the huge snake. But it continued to menace the god. It wasn't until Apollo had emptied his quiverful of arrows, one by one, into the scaly body that Python finally lay dead.

Knowing that nothing could stand before the son of Zeus, Themis took herself off, and Apollo was left in possession of this fairest spot on Earth. Here the Castalian spring would one day spill its purifying waters from a cleft in the mighty mountain to the stony basin below. From all the known world kings would come to lay their treasure at the feet of the oracle of Delphi and to receive its prophecies. A great temple arose at the base of the mountain, a temple to Apollo. Inside it was a stone marking the center of the world, while over its portal were two inscriptions reflecting the character of the god of light: "Know thyself" and "Nothing in excess."

To celebrate his victory over Python, Apollo established sacred games, which were called the Pythian Games after the serpent he had conquered. Each year the best athletes in Greece came to compete. The victors in these very early times were crowned with oak leaves, for the oak was sacred to Zeus. Later, laurel would crown the victors, but this plant was not yet known to either Apollo or the world.

Though Apollo was a god and a most important one, Zeus made him pay for his murder of Python, protector of the Titan Themis. He banished the young god to Arcadia for one year. It was during this exile that Apollo met his first love.

The Story of Daphne

Daphne was the beautiful daughter of the river Ladon in Arcadia. Everything about her was grace and loveliness. Though many men had been captivated by her charm, Daphne begged her father never to force her to marry.

"I wish to remain a virgin like the goddess Artemis," she told him. "I want only to be left free, a spear in my hand, to roam the woods and fields."

"Your very beauty will make that impossible," her father told her. "I can easily grant your wish not to force you to marry, but the young bloods of Arcadia will leave you no peace until you have chosen one of them."

"My swift feet and sharp spear will protect me from **any** of them," Daphne replied.

Henceforth surrounded by a troop of maidens who had taken similar vows to remain unmarried, Daphne roamed the woods, a maiden huntress like Artemis herself.

Not long before his exile, Apollo met Eros, son of Aphrodite. Though a mere child, Eros was armed with a small bow and a quiver of arrows.

Apollo smiled derisively at the sight of Eros. "What is a child like you doing with weapons that ape a man's? Behold my silver bow and the arrows that have killed mighty Python. Surely you do not take seriously such toys as those you carry."

"You may mock me as you please," said the little god of love, "but my arrows would have power over you if I should choose to use them."

Apollo laughed and turned away. It was then that Eros took a gold-tipped arrow from his quiver, fitted it to his bow, and shot it into Apollo. Victims of these arrows could not feel the darts, but they had the power to make the targets fall hopelessly in love with the first person they met of the opposite sex. At the same time, Eros fitted a lead-tipped arrow to his bow and, standing on the summit of Mount Parnassus, shot it straight across the gulf of Corinth and into the heart of Daphne in her Arcadian forest. This arrow would make the victim find anyone of the opposite sex repulsive.

Crossing the isthmus, Apollo descended into Arcadia, and the very first woman he met as he settled to Earth was Daphne. She was running wildly, trailed by her maidens. Her hair was blown back from her face, and her arms and legs were scratched by briers and bushes. Yet to Apollo's eyes she was the most beautiful mortal he had ever seen. Straightway he fell in love.

Daphne, turning at his glad cry, beheld the golden god shining with an unearthly brightness in the shadowy glade. Such loathing seized her that she was sick.

"Dear maiden," said Apollo, approaching her as she stood rooted with horror, "do not look so fearful. You are no less beautiful than my sister, Artemis. Therefore do not be afraid, for I am a god and I love you."

His words seemed to give Daphne sudden strength. She whirled and began to run. Her maidens tried to follow but were soon outdistanced. On and on they went along the forest aisles, Apollo racing after Daphne. For a while she managed to escape him, but then her strength began to fail. She stumbled once, and Apollo almost grasped her. It was then she cried out to her mother, Earth. "Save me, oh, save me quickly."

And Earth heard her cry. Even as Apollo's arms reached for her, a change came over Daphne. Her hands, stretched at arm's length before her, began to put forth leaves. Her feet were all at once rooted to the ground. A treelike bark began to enclose her soft body. All at once a laurel tree stood where there had been a frightened girl.

Apollo grasped the tree and pressed his brow against its trunk.

"Forever you will be sacred to me," he said.

And forever after the laurel (*daphne* in Greek) was sacred to Apollo, as the oak was to Zeus and the olive to Athena. Henceforth the victors in the Pythian games at Delphi received as their reward a crown of laurel, the choicest prize an athlete could win.

Apollo
and Hermes

Hermes, son of Zeus and the nymph Maia, was born in a cave in Arcadia. Following his birth, gentle Maia wrapped him lovingly in swaddling clothes and placed him in his cradle. But this was no ordinary infant; no cradle would hold him long.

Like any other healthy, newborn baby, Hermes slept peacefully for several hours. Around noon he wakened. It was dark and quiet in the cave. He looked about him. Off in a shadowy corner his mother lay sleeping. There was no one else around.

Very quietly Hermes slipped out of his swaddling clothes, climbed out of his cradle and, walking sturdily upright, approached the mouth of the cave where bright sunlight lay. It was noon, and the sun shone directly down upon him as he came out of his cave home. It felt good, and the baby god tipped up his face and lifted his arms to Apollo's fiery chariot blazing in the sky.

He took a few steps into the sunshine and caught sight of a tortoise making its slow way along the ground. Hermes stared in astonishment at the creature, then started toward it, laughing.

"Here is treasure," he exclaimed. "Come old fellow, I have plans for you."

Hermes seized the tortoise, and despite the poor thing's efforts to draw into its shell and save itself, the young god managed to kill it with merciful quickness. Next he ripped off its shell.

"This will make an excellent plaything," said the god, eyeing the shell speculatively. "It will become a joy to all mankind. This speckled shell shall be the highlight of every feast, a necessity of the dance, a treasure of the very gods."

Hermes immediately procured seven lengths of sheep gut, cut very thin. He strung these across the inner area of the shell, fastening the ends where it curved gently in upon itself. When he had done, he swept his fingers across the strings and a sweet sound came forth. Hermes had invented the lyre!

His first day's work accomplished, the precocious baby returned to his cradle, rolled himself up again in his swaddling clothes (the lyre hidden safely under them), and waited for his mother to find him.

When the sun's horses had descended the western sky and begun their long journey under ocean to the Gates of Dawn, Hermes became restive. He had lain in his cradle all afternoon and he was bored. Besides, the dark that lay beyond the cave's mouth intrigued the infant even as the sunlight had done earlier. Again he looked carefully about, and again he found Maia fast asleep. He could escape with perfect safety. This time he had a plan all worked out in his baby mind. It involved playing a trick upon the great Apollo. For all his golden might, Apollo would have to reckon with this small new brother. Hermes laughed softly as he left his cave.

The plan he had worked out was to steal the cattle of the golden god. This was no small feat since the herd was pastured on the slopes of Mount Olympus far off in Thessaly near the spring Pieria, dear to the Muses. It was a very long journey, from one end of Greece to the other. It would have taken a mounted army many days to make such a march. But then this was no ordinary infant!

In a remarkably short time, young Hermes was at the base of high Olympus and there, dark shadows against the night, moved the cattle. Quickly Hermes cut out fifty head, all of them the valued property of Apollo. Next he tossed off his sandals, and with moss and twigs and lengths of reed fashioned footgear in the shape of snowshoes. He fastened them to his feet backward so that their trailing ends were under his toes. With each step he took, his tracks showed him to be walking backward. Backward he drove the cattle, too, for mile upon mile.

When the moon began to climb the sky, Hermes and his herd came upon an old man at work in his vineyard. The man, amazed, watched the strange scene in silence. But when Hermes caught sight of the old man he hailed him in a voice that quite belied his size.

"Old man," cried the god, "if anyone should pass this way and ask if you have seen a herd of cattle, remember that you have seen nothing. Nothing at all. Do you hear?"

The old man nodded, unable to speak.

"Only remember," said Hermes, "or it will go ill with you."

He proceeded with the herd until he came to a large river, and here he sacrificed two heifers. After he had killed them, he rubbed two laurel sticks together, producing a spark that he let fall upon a heap of tinder. This was the first time that fire had been kindled in this way since Prometheus first gave it to man. And when the blaze was right, the young god dragged the slaughtered kine toward it and, so great was his strength, threw the carcasses upon the fire. The savory odor of the roasting meat soon filled the air, but Hermes, though hungry by this time, knew better than to eat it. His sacrifice was for the family on Mount Olympus, the family he hoped he and his mother might soon join.

When the sacrifice was completed, and the moon was going down in the west, Hermes drove the cattle at last into a meadow near the cave. Then entering his cave home silently, he went at once to his cradle, climbed into it, and tucked himself up snugly in his swaddling clothes, the picture of baby innocence.

But Maia was not fooled. Like any other mother, she knew full well when her errant son had come home. Moreover, she knew what he had been about, and now she warned him from her shadowy couch.

"Apollo, I fear, will make you pay most dearly for your theft of his cattle, my son."

Hermes laughed impertinently. "Oh, Mother, why bother to scold? I'm not like other children; this you know. I have a plan for us, and this night's work will further it. Do you want to spend your whole immortal life in this dark cave? Then leave off scolding me and trust my cleverness. Were I like other children, then you'd have something to worry about. Instead, I am a god, the god of thieves. Not even great Apollo can get the better of me. And if he tries, I'll steal everything he has, even his sacred tripod at Delphi on which his priestess sits to give out oracles."

So saying Hermes drifted off to sleep, but Maia tossed till dawn upon her couch.

And with the dawn, Leto's golden son came springing down the Olympian slopes to check his cattle. A shadow crossed the god's bright brow. What was this? He counted again. Fifty gone! It could not be! And yet it was. He searched the ground, but all the steps pointed toward Olympus. And what were these strange marks? Apollo stopped to study them more closely. He saw them plainly in the sand—webbed markings as if reeds crisscrossed a frame. But these, too, pointed toward the slopes where the cattle should be pastured and were not. What trick was this? Apollo straightened and gazed south as a certainty seized him. Then he was off, his arrows clanging in the quiver on his back.

The first person he met was the old man still at work in his vineyard. "Tell me, old man, did you see a herd of cattle go by here in the night? Fifty head have been stolen from my herd pastured near the spring Pieria."

The old man pondered this for a moment. He knew a god addressed him and he knew which god. But he also knew that the baby who had threatened him last night was no mortal child. Whom should he obey? Whom should he fear the most?

"Well, sir, the fact is," he began cautiously, "many pass by this vineyard in a day. Some I notice and some I never see as I bend my attention to my task. Yet it does seem to me that I remember last night seeing under the moon a child, a mere infant really, driving a herd of cattle backward. It seems unlikely that it could be true, so I may have dreamed it merely."

Apollo had heard enough and quickly continued on his way, his suspicions all confirmed. This brat was his father's youngest. Only Zeus could have sired such an infant, and Apollo knew where to find him. Soon he stood stooping in the cave's entrance, the sunlight bright behind him.

Hermes, peeping over the side of his cradle, beheld the god. He saw at once that his brother was furious, and for a brief moment even the impudent Hermes felt concern, for a god's wrath is fearful to behold. But confidence came quickly back to the little god of thieves, and he snuggled closer into his swaddling clothes, his beloved tortoise shell hidden safely under them.

Apollo strode to the crib. He looked down on the slyly sleeping baby. He looked all innocence, and Apollo smiled grimly. Then he sent his eagle's gaze around the large cavern. It might have held fifty cattle, but no cattle did he see. He turned back to the crib.

"You thieving rascal," cried the golden god. "Where are my kine? Tell me quickly or such a quarrel will grow between us as only our father Zeus can resolve." He reached in and gave the "sleeping" baby a shake. "Speak or I shall hurl you into Tartarus where you may dwell among the tortured gods. Where you may watch Sisyphus forever pushing his heavy stone up the unending hill and the damned Tantalus forever struggling to end his thirst. Such will be your fate little brother if you do not tell me at once where you have hidden my cows."

Hermes opened his eyes, wide and innocent. "Oh,
son of Leto, great Apollo, what madness brings you
here to seek your cattle? How could I have taken them?
I am but a baby one day old. I do not know what the
word *cattle* means." And Hermes stuck a thumb into
his mouth while his quite untroubled eyes attentively
studied the face looking down at him.

Apollo smiled, not ungently. "Cunning rogue, I see
it all now. So this is the gift the gods have given you. A
new god is before me, the god of thieves." Then his
face darkened. "But this I say to you, unless you want
this to be your last sleep, crawl out of that crib and
find my cows." Hermes continued to lie there sucking
his thumb. Suddenly Apollo reached in and, seizing
infant and swaddling clothes in one mighty hand,
lifted them up together and flung them on the turf
outside the cave. "Get up, you brat, and find my cattle,
or by the head of Zeus this will be your last thievery."

Hermes picked himself up and, reaching down,
drew his swaddling clothes up around him.

"You shameful god," he cried, dabbing at his eyes
where tears had formed. "What do you plan to do with
me? I haven't stolen your cattle. The gods would laugh
to hear you make such a claim. I am a little baby and
have never ever seen a cow."

So they argued, Apollo insisting, Hermes denying.
The golden god knew perfectly that the infant lied.
And yet he hardly dared, mighty as he was, to wring

this infant's neck as he desired to do. This was a son of Zeus.

At last they decided to lay the matter before their father, since neither could win over the other. Together they journeyed toward Olympus and at last stood before the throne of Zeus. All the Immortals came to witness the judgment.

Zeus studied his two sons with some amusement and at last spoke to Apollo.

"What has prompted you to bring this baby here before me? Whatever reason could involve such as he, it is far too trivial for a council of the gods."

"Not so, my father," said Apollo. "This little boy has stolen fifty head from my cattle herd and hidden them away. This I know with certain knowledge, yet he denies it all."

Before Zeus could reply, Hermes spoke. "Dear Father, how could such things be? Do I look like the kind of fellow who could drive off fifty head of cattle? I am a little newborn thing. Apollo is indeed great and admirable in all things, greatest among the gods after you, Father. Yet he did come to my abode yesterday and, leaning over my crib where I cowered in terror, did threaten me with dismal Tartarus unless I returned his stolen cattle. No doubt his cattle have been stolen, and it is a grievous thing that a god should suffer so. Only I swear that I am guiltless of the deed, as anyone who sees me should believe. Therefore I beg you, Father, to defend my babyhood and protect me from the wrath of your most glorious son."

Zeus had sunk his chin into his hand as he listened to the pleading of this his youngest son. Now he smiled around his hand and said, "Little liar, you cannot fool me. You stole the cattle and I know your purpose in stealing them. If you would achieve that purpose, then reveal to your brother his hidden herd or else you will never share with us the joys of high Olympus."

Now Hermes smiled, for in the words of Zeus he heard a veiled endorsement of his plan. He bowed, turned, then walked from the great hall. Apollo followed. Straight to the meadow where he had left the fifty cows Hermes led the way. And when Apollo saw his fifty kine he marveled that one so small could have achieved the theft. Then his brow darkened at the thought that anyone, even a son of Zeus, should have dared to play this trick upon him. Hermes noted that angry look and prepared to flee. Then another idea held him to the spot. He had taken up his lyre when first the two had started for Olympus. Not once had it left his hand, and now to soothe his brother's anger he struck some chords upon it.

Apollo, who had never heard anything like these sounds, forgot his cattle and listened with all his heart. Then Hermes lifted up his voice in song, and as the lyre played on he told of the adventures of the gods. He sang of Leto's wanderings, and Apollo was filled

with sorrow. He sang of the special glories of each of
the Immortals and Apollo rejoiced to hear. At last the
song ended.

"You little schemer, where did you learn such music? Was it born in you like your gift to steal? Such
glorious sounds are worth the price of all my cattle.
Therefore take these you stole last night and let me
have in return that instrument on which you have just
played." Apollo's face was full of joy as he spoke, and
he stretched out a hand to receive the lyre. "But give
it me and I swear I will myself escort you and your
mother, gentle Maia, to high Olympus and there in-
stall you both as worthy inmates of that place, there to
dwell forever in the company of the Immortals."

"Great Apollo, I know the gifts Zeus has bestowed
on you. Prophecy, healing, and all wisdom are yours.
Therefore take this lyre and add the gift of music to
your great store of riches." Hermes gave the lyre into
Apollo's hand. The god struck it, and such music rose
from it as brought the gods rushing to the edge of
Mount Olympus, where they leaned listening to the
ravishing sounds. Nymphs and dryads left their streams
and trees to dance to the glad measures, and shepherds
tending their flocks noted how the animals ceased their
restless roamings and lay down, chewing their cuds
while the sweet music flowed around them.

Then the two godly brothers each swore by the river
Styx to respect and love each other. Never again would

Hermes steal from Apollo, and never again would the golden god seek to do the other harm. In witness of their oaths, Apollo gave to Hermes a magic wand, which would be useful to him when later he became the messenger of Zeus. The fifty cattle, too, Apollo gave him, and they drove that herd to the Pierian spring where it was mingled with the other herds.

So at last Hermes and his mother came to Mount Olympus where they lived forever after. And who can say whether it was trickery or inventiveness that won them that high abode?

Apollo and Pan

One day Pan met Apollo on a mountain in Phrygia. The golden god was strumming his lyre.

"Those twanging strings cannot compete with the notes I make upon my pipes," Pan said to Apollo in greeting him. It was Pan who had invented the syrinx and piped its music through meadow and wood.

"There are those who would not agree with you," Apollo answered him. "No sound in all the earth is as sweet as my music."

"Since we disagree, let us hold a contest with a judge to decide between us," said Pan, who was half goat, half man.

Apollo willingly agreed.

The mountain on which the two gods met contained a deity whose name was Tmolos. They called

him forth and asked him to listen and judge whether Pan's pipes or Apollo's lyre gave off the sweeter sounds.

Apollo played first. The leaves hung silent on the trees, and every bird stopped singing to hear his magic sound. Then Pan put his pipes to his mouth and blew a tune so clear and lively that the water within a little stream near them slowed its rushing and moved silently around the rocks, the better to listen to the gentle piping.

When Pan had finished, Tmolos sat a moment in silence while the two musicians watched him tensely.

"No sound of Earth or heaven could be as sweet as your music, Apollo," Tmolos said at last. "I name you the winner of this contest."

Apollo had time only to flash a look of triumph at Pan, who stamped his goat's feet in rage and humiliation, before another came upon the scene. This was King Midas who, concealed within the grove, had heard the music.

"I, too, heard the contest," he now declared, "and I disagree with the decision. Pan is the winner."

Immediately the bright face of Apollo darkened. "Those are dangerous words, Midas," he warned. "Withdraw them or you will regret you ever spoke."

But Midas refused.

And while he stood stubbornly arguing Pan's cause, his ears began to grow. Up and up the sides of his head they rose until they towered well above it. Fur covered them inside and out. Midas's face was framed between two donkey's ears.

"Since your musical taste is no better than a donkey's, wear a donkey's ears," said Apollo and stalked away.

Ashamed, Midas sneaked back to his palace holding the long ears doubled over on either side of his head. He managed to reach his bedroom without anyone seeing him, and there, horrified at what his mirror revealed, he arranged a large turban around his head so as to cover the ears completely.

But there was one from whom he could not hide them. This was his barber. The good man was much astonished when he discovered what the turban was hiding.

"Swear that you will never reveal this to a soul," demanded Midas.

The barber readily swore. But the need to confide the secret to *someone* so nagged the barber that at last he gave in to it. Knowing it would be worth his life to share the king's secret with any human being, he went from the palace to where a little stream meandered through a meadow. He knelt down beside a clump of reeds that grew beside the stream.

"Listen," he whispered to the reeds. "King Midas has donkey's ears."

At once the reeds took up the words and repeated them over and over. "King Midas has donkey's ears."

To this very day you may hear the reeds whispering
those words whenever a wind moves through them.
And ever since barbers have often been accused of
being gossips.

Apollo's Revenge and Punishment

CORONIS

Apollo was unlucky in his loves. Coronis, one of these, was pregnant with his child when she very foolishly allowed herself to fall in love with a mortal. The god might never have known of her betrayal except for the crow. This bird, Apollo's messenger, eagerly reported to the god that Coronis was untrue.

Apollo's rage was frightful to behold. Seizing his bow, he descended upon Thessaly, where Coronis lived. He found her walking in her father's garden, and without a second thought he sent an arrow into her breast. Coronis fell, and her blood poured out upon the garden path.

Then remorse seized Apollo. "Ah, my love," he cried, "why did I give way to passion?"

He took her limp body into his arms and tried to
breathe life back into her. But not even the god of
healing could restore the unfortunate girl to life.

Meanwhile the crow, well-satisfied with what it had
done, perched on the branch of a nearby lime tree and
began pluming its white feathers. Apollo saw the bird,
and again fury shook him. But for that miserable crow
and its tattling tongue Coronis would be alive.

"Accursed bird," cried the god, "you shall be punished for this death. That all men may be reminded
of your meddling ways, from this day forth your
feathers shall be black."

In the next moment, where had sat a bird as white
as sea mist, there appeared a bird whose dark feathers
matched the tree's dark shadows on the ground.

Before the body of Coronis was placed upon its funeral pyre, Apollo took her unborn child from it, a
son. He carried the baby over mountain and plain until he came to the abode of the good centaur, Cheiron.

Centaurs were strange and raucous creatures, half
horse and half man. Their bodies were those of powerful stallions, but from the shoulders of these stallions
rose the torsos of men. The centaurs were rough and
lawless, all except Cheiron, who was wise and good.
He lived in a cave on Mount Pelion and had reared
Jason, among other heroes. Now he was to become the
mentor of Apollo's infant son, Asclepius.

In keeping with Apollo's office as god of healing, the

all-wise Cheiron instructed Asclepius in the art of medicine. By the time he had sons and daughters of his own, Apollo's son was a renowned physician, famed throughout the known world and worshiped everywhere. Into modern times physicians upon entering their profession took the Hippocratic oath, which begins, "I swear by Apollo the physician, by Asclepius, by Hygieia, by Panacea [daughters of Asclepius], and by all the gods and goddesses. . . ."

But the day came when Asclepius proved too clever for his own good. He raised a man from the dead. Zeus was angered. To cure ills was one thing; to raise men from the dead betokened a power no mere mortal should have. Zeus hurled a thunderbolt at Asclepius and killed him.

When Apollo learned of his great son's death, his rage matched that of Zeus. But though a powerful god in his own right, there was nothing Apollo could do against the might of the All-Father. Still he would have his revenge, and he took it against the Cyclopes, who had made the thunderbolt that struck down Asclepius.

The Cyclopes were three rude giants, each having a single eye in the very middle of his forehead. Sometimes they lived as shepherds, herding their flocks and returning at night to huge caves where they lived and stored the produce of their flocks and fields. At other times they worked with Hephaestus, god of the forge,

in his workshop under the volcanic Mount Etna. It must have been here that they fashioned the thunderbolts for Zeus before Apollo took his revenge upon them for the death of Asclepius, and killed them with his arrows.

Not even his own son could murder a servant of Zeus with impunity, and so Apollo had to be punished for killing the Cyclopes.

At first Zeus thought to banish the golden god to Tartarus, that dark region lower than Hades where the vanquished Titans and the wickedest of mortals suffered eternal punishment. But Leto begged mercy for her son, and Zeus relented. Apollo was sentenced to serve a mortal man as his serf for one year. It was a humiliating sentence.

Fortunately for the god, the mortal whom Zeus chose for his son's master was King Admetus of Pherae. He was a just and kindly man and welcomed the herdsman who came to him seeking work and food. So considerate was the king's treatment that Apollo was moved to reward him. Suddenly the king's herds began to increase. Ewes and mares and cows gave birth to twins. All the young were sturdy and grew rapidly. Admetus was amazed at the good luck his new herdsman had brought him, never dreaming, of course, that it was the god of flocks himself who watched over the grazing herds.

THE WOOING OF ALCESTIS

It happened that about the time Apollo became his herdsman, Admetus was hopeful of winning the hand of a daughter of King Pelias of Iolcus. This was the same King Pelias who had sent Jason in quest of the Golden Fleece. Indeed, Admetus had been one of the heroes aboard *Argo*. Returning from that adventure, he had fallen deeply in love with the beautiful Alcestis, whose beauty was only excelled by her goodness. There were so many suitors for her hand that her father said at last that he would give her in marriage to that man who could yoke a lion and a boar to a chariot.

The task seemed utterly preposterous. Surely, thought Admetus, the old king must want his daughter to live and die husbandless.

One day he spoke of his hopeless love to his new herdsman, with whom he had become unusually friendly.

"If you will give me leave to go from you for three days," said his herdsman, "and will promise to meet me in Iolcus at the end of that time, you may claim your bride."

Admetus smiled at this bravado. And yet he admired the herdsman's courage and was touched by his evident concern.

"So be it," declared Admetus. "For three days another shall watch my flocks while you go about your business whatsoever it may be. I shall await you in Iolcus."

They parted and the herdsman went across the meadow and out of sight. Admetus watched him go, a wondering smile upon his lips. Was this herdsman more than he appeared to be? There was, after all, that sudden increase in the flocks. Musing, Admetus returned to his palace.

Three days later there was a stir in that same marketplace where Jason had first greeted King Pelias. Again a stranger stood there facing the crowd. This man was plainly a herdsman. He held a struggling beast in either hand. One was a boar with savage eyes and menacing tusks. The other was a lion that snarled, revealing long white fangs.

"Summon King Admetus," said the herdsman. A man left the crowd and darted off in the direction of the palace.

When Admetus, answering the summons, saw what awaited him in the marketplace, his face lighted with hope and joy. He ordered a chariot brought at once. By the time it had arrived, Pelias had joined the group.

"It means nothing that this fellow has procured two beasts," he informed his prospective son-in-law. "You, yourself, must yoke them to the chariot, Admetus."

"Here," said the herdsman, offering to Admetus the tethers by which the animals were held. "Take them and yoke them. They will do your bidding."

Admetus seized the tethers and led the wild beasts toward the waiting chariot. They went quietly, and he ranged them on either side of the chariot pole and yoked it to their necks. It sagged down sharply on the side of the boar, but Pelias had said nothing about driving the pair.

Admetus turned to Pelias with a look of triumph. "Alcestis is mine, O king. I have performed the task you required. The wild beasts are yoked."

An approving murmur rose from the crowd, and Pelias slowly nodded his head. "The marriage shall be celebrated forthwith," he declared.

And so it was. But in the joy and excitement of the marriage festival, Admetus forgot to make the traditional offering to Artemis, goddess of the hunt. Since all wild things were under her protection, Admetus should have given thanks for the use he had made of her boar and lion. Therefore when that night he and Alcestis retired to their chamber, they found it full of snakes, an evil omen.

Apollo served his sentence while Artemis bided her time. She waited until Admetus and Alcestis had been married a few happy years, rejoicing in their love and the children of that love, before she struck.

THE REVENGE OF ARTEMIS

Artemis worked subtly to avenge herself against Admetus. She could quite easily have killed him with an arrow shot from her golden bow. Instead, she approached the Moerae, or Fates, and elicited their help in ridding the world of her wrongdoer.

The Fates were three dreary crones named Clotho, Lachesis, and Atropos. Like all old women of that time, these were spinners. But they were as much unlike ordinary spinners as they were unlike any other old women. Clotho, Lachesis, and Atropos were daughters of Night, and their labors decided what each mortal's portion of life would be. Clotho it was who spun the thread of life, Lachesis who measured it, and Atropos who cut it when the measure was reached.

Artemis had no difficulty in persuading the Fates to terminate the life of Admetus. A powerful goddess, a daughter of Zeus, she had been slighted by a mortal so beguiled by his own happiness he had forgotten the gods. The Fates were all too ready to deal with such a one.

But now once again Apollo played a crucial hand in his former master's affairs. Somehow he learned of what the Fates intended doing with the life-span of

Admetus. Perhaps the same crow who had tattled on Coronis saw a chance to redeem himself by warning Apollo of the fate in store for the king. At any rate, the golden god lost no time in seeking out the Fates. They were flattered by this attention, for even the gods avoided the dismal trio. And when the god invited them to his mansion for a feast, their withered faces came as near to lighting as it was possible for them to do.

It was a strange banquet. At the head of the table sat Apollo, shining and splendid, and ranged around the board were the three crones, their long thin noses reaching down their gray faces almost to their thin, unsmiling lips. But their host maintained the very best of cheer. He urged upon them the delicious viands and, most important, he kept their goblets filled with wine. The old women had never enjoyed such hospitality, and they ate—and drank—heartily. When the god had decided that enough wine had been consumed to meet his purpose, he spoke of what was on his mind.

"I have lately learned," he began, "that you plan the death of a friend of mine."

"You have countless friends, Apollo," said Atropos. "Surely each day some must die."

"True," agreed Apollo. "But this is a particular friend. He is kind and just, a good master, a loving husband, and a wise father."

"Who is this miraculous mortal?" asked Lachesis.

"King Admetus of Pherae," answered Apollo.

"Not even Zeus can change a decision of the Fates," Clotho announced.

"True again," declared Apollo. "But the Fates themselves can change it." He again reached to fill the goblets. "Now I urge in the name of justice to let Admetus live."

"He has forfeited that right," said Clotho. "He grossly slighted your own sister, Artemis. He forgot the gods on his wedding day."

"I know all that," said Apollo. "Yet there is something to be said for Admetus. So intense was his joy at winning his longed-for bride that he could think of nothing else. I, too, have known love, and so I can understand how Admetus felt. But my sister could in no wise understand this. She is a virgin sworn and looks with loathing on romantic love. She could no more feel compassion for Admetus than she could rejoice in his happiness."

The Fates listened to his words while they sipped Apollo's wine. A little color had come into their gray cheeks, softening their stern faces. Apollo noted it with satisfaction; perhaps the wine had softened their hearts as well.

At length Atropos spoke. "We cannot cancel out the sentence already passed on Admetus, but we can offer a compromise. If the king can find someone to die in his place, we will let him live. Otherwise, he must descend to Hades where Pluto awaits him."

The other two nodded in agreement with their sister's words, and Apollo had to be content with this arrangement.

ADMETUS SEEKS A SUBSTITUTE

Apollo lost no time in telling Admetus what the Fates had in store for him. He found the king seated in a sun-dappled arbor within the palace garden. With an amused smile he was watching his three small children playing at his feet. Suddenly the sunlight within the arbor brightened, and out of that brightness Apollo spoke.

"Admetus your fate has been decided. Unless you can find someone to die in your place, Hades will claim you in three days' time. It is Apollo who brings you this warning."

The face of the king paled as he heard the awful words. His mouth was suddenly so dry he could scarcely speak.

"What have I done that the gods should cut short my life at the very peak of its strength and joy?"

"You forgot to make sacrifice to Artemis on your wedding day," said the voice out of the brightness. "She filled your bridal chamber with snakes, and now she will have her final revenge for your slight to her. Find someone to take your place in Pluto's halls or be ready when Thanatos, the god of death, comes to lead you there."

It was a while after the brightness vanished before Admetus found the strength to leave the arbor. His steps were halting, like those of an aged man, but the children ran gaily after their father, not knowing of the calamity to be visited upon their house.

Admetus called a council of his chiefs and had the news of his impending death announced throughout his kingdom. Great was the consternation and the mourning. Being just and kind, he was popular with his subjects. Surely there would be no want of volunteers to take his place in Hades. So the king thought. But the first day passed, and the second, and no one came forward to die in the king's place.

On the third day he confided to Alcestis his intention of appealing to his parents. She encouraged him. "Surely your mother would give her life for yours."

Hopefully Admetus sought his parents' apartment in the palace.

"Dear Mother," he began when she had dismissed her handmaiden, "you are old and infirm. And a woman. Your days are numbered. Perhaps your very hours. The Fates have decreed that I must die at once unless someone will die for me. You gave me life. I beseech you now to preserve it by dying in my stead."

His mother wept as she listened to his words and wrung her hands. Her reply came haltingly. "You ask too much, my son. It is true my life may end at any moment. Yet each instant is sweet. I have no wish to join the shades in Hades until Atropos shall cut my life's thread."

Admetus turned to his father. "You are a man and brave," he told him, "but useless now. It has been years since you gave over the kingdom to me. I am its ruler and its mainstay. Who knows what its fortunes will be if I am gone? You, too, are old—older than my mother—and your life may end at any moment. You know the importance of a king; for the sake of our dynasty then, submit to dying in my place."

But his father shook his head. "We have only one life to live and the light is sweet. I have no wish to face the dark halls of Hades before my time. I have given you life and honor and riches. It is not required that I should give you my life as well."

"Coward," cried Admetus. "From this moment I disown you as my father. Nor can she longer be my mother. You two will live out your short days rich in the contempt of men. And when you die you will be buried without honor."

Gathering his royal robes about him, Admetus stormed out of their presence and sought his wife. One look at his face, and she knew of his parents' refusal. For a moment indecision looked out of her own. Then she drew herself up proudly.

"Fear no longer, Admetus. Your wife will die for you."

With a cry, Admetus swept her into his arms. "Dear

Alcestis, you are as brave as you are beautiful. What dreadful curse is on us that you should be torn from me who loves you so well? Were I not king, you should not make this sacrifice."

Alcestis freed herself. "Indeed I understand, Admetus. What man could ever take your place upon your throne? What is a woman that she should value her life above her husband's?" Suddenly her lovely face crumpled and tears flowed down her cheeks. "Yet I too love life. And I am loath to leave it before my little children have grown beyond a mother's care. One thing promise me, my husband."

"But ask it," said Admetus. "I swear to grant anything you wish, my dear one."

"It is this: that you will never marry until our children are grown. Promise me that no other woman shall take my place and make my children suffer to the advantage of her own."

"There shall be no wife of mine again within this house. Nor any feasting or revelry. With you gone, there will be a blight upon my life. Our children must be the recompense for your loss, my Alcestis. And when my life has run its full course, we shall share the same grave bed. There I shall join you again to love you through all eternity."

Alcestis made no reply, but turned away from him to summon her handmaidens and prepare herself for death. First she arrayed herself in her most beautiful gown. Next she opened a chest filled with jewelry fash-

ioned from the gold of Egypt. She slid golden brace-
lets up her white arms. Around her slender neck she
looped coils of yellow gold. Jeweled earrings dangled
from her small ears, just showing below the soft hair
held neatly by golden hairpins. When all had been
completed, she called her children to her. They were
too young to understand her tears.

"Mother, you look so grand! Is there a festival today?" asked the little boy.

Alcestis shook her head, too moved for speech.

The little girls looked wonderingly upon her finery.
Shyly they lifted the loops of the necklace in their
chubby hands. "Pretty," they said in chorus.

With a sob, Alcestis threw her arms around them
and held them close. "Oh, my children, it is pain to
know that you will forget me. You are so little. What
will your lives be without a mother to love and care
for you?" She lifted swimming eyes to Admetus. "Now
you must be father and mother to them," she said.
"Let them hear my name and know they had a mother
who loved them. And let you never forget, Admetus,
that I loved you better than life."

Suddenly she reached out for him. "Hold me," she
cried. "I can no longer stand. Charon is approaching.
I can see him in his little boat. This is the moment,
Admetus. Now I am dying. Farewell."

She became limp in his arms, and he carried her to
a couch and gently lowered her upon it. Bending, he
pressed an ear against her breast. She was dead.

The sorrowful news sped quickly. A pitiful wailing began, its volume increasing until it filled the palace even to the slaves' quarters. Alcestis had been greatly loved. Never was mistress so kind; never was wife so true.

THE ARRIVAL OF HERACLES

Suddenly above the mournful chorus a voice sounded from the courtyard.

"Ho, within the house! Is Admetus at home?"

A slave hurried out to find a huge man waiting in the courtyard, travel stained and weary, wearing a lion-skin and carrying a club.

"Is King Admetus at home?" repeated Heracles, for it was he, the mightiest hero of Greece.

"He is even now approaching," said the slave as Admetus stepped from the palace.

"Greetings, Admetus."

"Welcome to Pherae, Heracles," said the king.

Heracles lowered his club and took a step forward. In a somewhat subdued voice he asked, "Why are you in mourning Admetus? Why has your slave cut his hair? I heard loud wailing as I approached the palace."

"Someone dear to me has died and must be buried this day," returned Admetus sadly.

"Not one of the children?"

Admetus shook his head. "No kinsman of mine," he said.

"A man or woman?" asked Heracles.

"A woman," replied Admetus.

"She must have been wellborn to be so mourned. How, then, did she come to die within your house?"

"Losing her father, she sought a home here."

"I respect your sorrow and shall seek hospitality somewhere else, Admetus."

"What senseless talk is this?" demanded Admetus. "You will stay on as my guest. The dead shall in no way alter your claim upon me. We have guest quarters, and you are always welcome in them."

"When there is mourning a friend is in the way," protested Heracles. "I beseech you, let me go."

Admetus turned to the slave, who had remained at a respectful distance. "You there," he said. "Prepare a guest chamber and see to it that my friend does not lack for food and drink."

Heracles crossed the courtyard with the slave to the guest quarters opposite. Admetus turned and was about to re-enter the palace when one of his aged councilors approached him.

"Admetus, forgive my words if I speak too boldly. But I am old and advised your father before I began counseling you." The old man halted. At a sign from the king he continued. "It would appear that grief has warped your sense of fitness. This is no time to entertain your friends."

"This is my best friend," declared Admetus, "whose hospitality never failed me when I sought his roof in Argos. Would it have lightened my sorrow had I turned him away? Rather would I have suffered for my inhospitality along with my grief."

The wise old man looked long at the young king, and a new respect for his monarch was in his gaze.

"Admetus, already your reputation for justness is well known. But now you have shown yourself to be truly noble. Only good can come to Pherae with such a king as you."

A few minutes later, the body of Alcestis was borne out of the palace, followed by Admetus, his court, and the servants. Hardly had they crossed the courtyard and disappeared from sight when the slave who had escorted Heracles came hurrying across from the guest quarters.

"Of all the people Admetus has entertained here, this is the worst guest of them all," he grumbled to himself since there was no one around to hear him. "In the first place, whoever he is, he should never have stayed here even though the master urged him to do so. He could see we were in deep mourning. And now he seems to have brushed off all consideration of the grief we were so plainly showing. He insists on what he wants in the way of food and drink. And as to the latter, he has consumed enough to make him drunk as Silenus at his worst."

The last words were scarcely spoken when Heracles came roaring out of the guest quarters quite plainly the worse for wine. Catching sight of the slave he shouted, "Why do you wear a long face? Here is a guest to entertain; this is no time for melancholy. Death we must face each day. And what is one more death? All life is chance. Therefore be happy while you can."

"There is no way I can find happiness this day," returned the slave. "I suffer from a deep and sudden grief. Any sign of joy would be out of place here today."

"It strikes me that your grief is out of bounds," continued Heracles. "A woman is dead, true. But she is no blood of this house. 'Tis not as if Admetus had lost his parents or his children or his wife."

The slave hesitated to reply then looked levelly at Heracles. "My lord, it is his wife. Our mistress, Alcestis, is dead." His voice broke on the last word.

The dread words sobered Heracles. He gasped, then eyed the slave menacingly. "Your words are enough to drape the world in mourning, if they be true. If you are lying, slave, I shall strangle you forthwith."

"I do not lie," replied the slave tonelessly. "Alcestis is dead."

Heracles shook his head savagely as if to clear it. "I should have known," he moaned. "I should have

known when I beheld the tears in Admetus's eyes, his
mourning clothes, and his shorn locks. Ah me, that my
wits might match my muscle! While that good man
concealed his painful loss, I have enjoyed his hospitality, drinking his wine and even wreathing my head
with vine leaves." He paused, considering. "Tell me,
where is the funeral being held?"

"Down the Larrisa road," answered the slave. "You
will see the mound when you have cleared the city
gates."

"Now," declared Heracles, more to himself than to
his listener, "I have a mission to perform. I must repay
Admetus for his kindness. Perhaps I can yet save Alcestis. I must go to her tomb and there await the god of
death."

HERACLES WINS A PRIZE

Heracles delayed only long enough to don his lionskin
and seize his club, and then he withdrew from the
palace

Beyond the city gates rose a mound in the shape of a
beehive. An entrance had been opened in one side of
the mound, which was lined with huge stones sitting
so tightly one upon another that no mortar was needed
to keep them in place. Low at the start, the sides of the
entrance rose toward the center of the mound, where

a tall doorway marked the end of the passageway. Here a massive stone, tall as the doorway, rested at one side waiting to be shoved along its track and into place.

With a quick look around, Heracles entered the darkness of the mound. He placed himself at one side of the doorway and waited. Off in the gloom, under the towering beehive roof where it curved to meet itself, stood a bier and on it the motionless body of Alcestis.

He had not long to wait. There was a rustle of great wings, and a sudden darkness cut off what light fell through the doorway. Thanatos had arrived to claim his own.

As he moved within the doorway, Heracles sprang and grasped him in his giant arms. Thanatos struggled, but to no avail. Heracles held him fast.

"You shall not approach her," he panted. "This day shall death be denied, Thanatos. This day shall hospitality be rewarded, and a noble wife returned to her husband."

As if proving his words, Heracles tightened his grip upon the god of death, and he felt Thanatos grow suddenly quiet in his arms.

"Enough, Heracles. Take her, if so you wish," said Thanatos. "The issue is merely postponed, in any case," he added darkly. "Finally she must come to me."

Heracles released him and stood back. Dark Death shook out his leathery wings and departed. Heracles crossed to the bier and lifted Alcestis in his arms.

Returned from the funeral, Admetus, his court, and
all his servants had surrendered themselves to grief.
The children, too, were now aware that something was
wrong and, seeking to be comforted, demanded their
mother. For the first time in their lives she had failed
to come when wanted, and indignation mingled with
their bewilderment.

"Alas, my poor children, your mother has gone
from you and through no wish of her own," Admetus
told them. But the words meant nothing to them.
Their whimpering rose to full-throated yells of pro-
test, and their nurses, struggling to subdue them,
carried them away.

It was then that a shout arose in the courtyard. Heracles had returned. At his side, her hand in his, walked
a woman heavily veiled, but moving with such languid
grace it was easy to see that she was young. Admetus
and those around him gazed with astonishment at the
approaching giant and the veiled and silent woman.

"Behold, Admetus, the prize I have won," he bel-
lowed. "I have brought her here to you for I must make
a journey to Thrace. She is yours to keep; I won her
fairly."

"I want her not," said Admetus. "It grieves me just
to look upon her, she moves so like my Alcestis."

"Yet take her," urged Heracles. "You cannot con-
tinue forever to sorrow for your lost wife."

Admetus's face hardened. "I did ill to keep my
sorrow from you, Heracles, for you were my dearest

friend. But now I resent your words. No woman can ever comfort me for the loss of my dear wife. Therefore take this one away."

Heracles smiled. "Your love for your lost wife does you honor, Admetus. But do not reject what the gods send. Here is a woman they have sent you. Put out your hand."

"I would as soon touch a Gorgon," said Admetus drawing back.

"Put out your hand," roared Heracles.

Slowly, shrinkingly, Admetus extended his right hand. Heracles laid that of the woman in it. At the same time he twitched off her long veil. The king let out a cry as did all the onlookers.

"Is this some cruel joke the gods have played on me?" cried Admetus. "Have I not suffered enough? Must they now mock me with the very image of my dead wife?"

"You feel her hand, Admetus," Heracles reminded him. "Is it the hand of a corpse, or do you feel the life-blood pulsing in it? This is indeed your wife, your own Alcestis. I fought Thanatos for her and won. Did I not say I won her as a prize?" His laugh shook the hall.

Wondering, Admetus took Alcestis in his arms. "Dear one, that you should be returned to me from the grave!" Over her head his eyes sought Heracles. "May good fortune always go with you, my friend. You will never want a friend while I live."

He held Alcestis at arm's length and looked long

into her eyes. A shadow came into his own, and he
turned to Heracles.

"Why is she so silent? Does she regret her return? If
she is glad to feel again my touch upon her, why does
she not speak and give some sign of it?"

"She has duties to the gods below in Hades who
have been cheated of their victim," explained Heracles. "Until the third morning after this return she
may not speak. After that, the kind words will again
come from her lips." He took up his club and tossed
it onto his shoulder, at the same time giving a hitch
to the lionskin. "So, then, farewell, Admetus, most
hospitable of kings. I will stop to share your happiness
on my return from Thrace. And the gods know when
that will be." Turning, he strode from the hall and out
of the palace and out of sight.

The House
of the Sun

Of all the palaces on Mount Olympus, Apollo's was
the most splendid. Its golden walls gave off a light as
brilliant as the sun, while the jewels ornamenting
those walls flashed and glowed. The whole palace
shone with a brilliance that dazzled the eyes. Its great
doors of gleaming silver had been fashioned by Hephaestus, god of the forge. On their shining surface
were engravings of the seas embracing Earth, Earth
itself, and all the gods who lived there. As well as the
gods of sea and Earth, there were pictured the spirits
that inhabited trees and streams, the dryads and
nymphs. Cities and their mortal inhabitants were also
shown, while over all arched the bright sky. Each of
the great double doors also bore the six signs of the
zodiac.

Here, deep within this shining palace, were stabled the horses of the sun. Each morning at the awakening of Dawn within her chamber, the horses were yoked to the fiery chariot. Then Apollo would drive the chariot out from the Gates of Dawn up into the sky and straight across the heavens until at last he reached the spot where his course descended into the western ocean and Night arrived. During the long hours of darkness, the horses traveled under the earth until at last they came to where the earth and sky met in the east. This marked the end of their journey, and they were led into the house of the sun through the Gates of Dawn to await the morrow's starting forth again.

When Apollo was not driving his horses across the sky or visiting the haunts of men, he often held court in his glittering palace. Then he wore the shining diadem upon his head that he wore when he was driving his chariot. His robe was purple and his throne encrusted with emeralds. Around him stood the members of his court: Day, Month, Year, and all the Hours in their appointed places. Spring wore a garland of flowers, Summer carried a sheaf of wheat, Autumn's feet were stained from treading out the grapes for wine, and Winter's gray locks were stiff with frost.

Here Apollo the sun god ruled his court, and the Hours did his bidding.

A CRUCIAL QUESTION

Clymene, who lived in Egypt, had one son whose name was Phaethon. His paternity was a mystery.

While he was small, it mattered not at all to Phaethon that no one ever mentioned his father. But the day came when he demanded to know whose son he was. The answer astonished him.

"Your father is Apollo, god of the sun," Clymene told him.

When next the boys at school taunted him for not knowing who his father was, Phaethon was ready for them.

"My father is none other than the god Apollo. My own mother told me so."

At this the boys jeered him more cruelly than ever. "A likely story," said one.

"Have you heard?" asked another. "I am a son of Zeus!"

This prompted each one of them to choose a god for sire, sniggering among themselves while Phaethon stood by, anger and humiliation reddening his cheeks.

Suddenly a brave determination seized him. His

eyes lighted with its challenge. He would go to the sun god's palace and ask Apollo himself whether or not Clymene had spoken truthfully. If so, then he would demand proof of it. He'd show these mocking boys! This would be the last time they would make fun of him, because Phaethon believed his mother had spoken the truth.

So without a word to anyone, he started for high Olympus and the palace of the sun. It was a long journey, but at last the boy stood within sight of the palace. Its brilliance nearly blinded him. Several times he had to stop and cover his eyes. But he continued bravely on, for his question must be answered one way or another. And only Apollo could give that answer.

Reaching the entrance to the throne room, Phaethon stopped to look within. Apollo was seated on his throne with his court around him and the shining diadem on his head. The boy had not long to wait, for the sun, who sees everything, soon noticed him.

"What has brought you to this lofty dwelling place, my lad?" asked Apollo.

Phaethon approached him boldly. "I have a question to ask you," he said. "A question only you can answer."

Apollo smiled at the seriousness of the boy's face. "Ask your question then," he said, removing the diadem from his head so that the boy's eyes would no longer be dazzled by it.

"My mother, Clymene, has told me that you are my father. But when I told this to my playmates at school, they made fun of me. So I have come to ask you if this be true and, if so, to give me proof of it."

Apollo reached out his arms and drew Phaethon into them. "Your mother, Clymene, has indeed spoken truthfully, my son. I swear I am your father, Phaethon. To prove it, you may ask anything of me you desire, and I swear by the Styx it will be granted you."

Phaethon had his answer ready. All during his long journey to the house of the sun he had considered what he would ask as proof if Apollo should claim him for his own. It did not take him long to decide what that proof should be. He knew of the sun god's drive across the sky each day in the fiery chariot drawn by the four fire-breathing horses. He knew how all the world watched and waited to see it leave the Gates of Dawn and mount the sky bringing heat and light to all below. So now he cried, "I ask that you let me drive your chariot for this one day. Just this one day."

At the words, the god's bright face darkened. How he repented his rash promise! Why had he so recklessly bound himself to grant whatever wish might spring into this boy's young head? If only the promise might be broken! Since this was impossible, then he would talk with the youngster. Perhaps he could make him see reason, thought Apollo.

"Dear lad," he began, "this is the thing I would

have refused you. All the world knows no one can drive my horses but me—all but you, alas. Not even Zeus can drive my chariot, and who is greater than the hurler of thunderbolts? What you ask for requires a skill beyond your strength and years. Let us first talk of the road. It is steep, so steep that though they are fresh and rested in the morning, the horses can hardly make their way up it. Then it rises so high into the heavens that when it reaches the zenith even I am frightened to see the earth so far below me. Finally, when the way slopes down, a strong hand is needed on the reins. The descent is so steep that even the sea nymphs fear for me. And all the while the sky is spinning, and the stars are spinning with it in dizzying circles. I manage to drive against the spin.

"But suppose you had my chariot? Could you keep to the course with the sky spinning and the earth whirling below you? And that isn't all. Monsters lie along your path: the Bull, the Lion, the Scorpion, and the Crab. To say nothing of the horses themselves, who are full of fire and fight all effort to control them. But they know I am their master; they must obey. Do you, then, think they will obey you? Beware lest I bestow on you a tragic gift. You want proof that I am your father. Surely I prove it by fearing for you as I do. Look into my face. How I wish you might look as well into my heart and know the awful concern I have for you, my son!

"Look around you. Think of all that the world holds and all the good things that could be yours from Earth and sea and sky. Ask and they shall be yours. Only this one thing do not ask of me. It is not a gift but a punishment you ask for."

Thus he ended his warning. And it did no good. Phaethon insisted that his father fulfill the oath. So, sorrowing, Apollo led him to where the chariot waited for the awakening of Dawn.

Again Hephaestus had fashioned a thing of great beauty. The chariot was of solid gold inlaid with ivory and set with gems. The rims of the wheels were gold and their spokes silver.

While Phaethon was staring in wonder at the car he was so soon to drive, Dawn wakened in her chamber. She threw wide her doors, and at once the stars began to pale. The horns of the crescent moon began to fade as all the sky turned rose. Apollo, noticing these signs, ordered the Hours to bring the horses. Quickly they led them from their stalls and yoked them to the waiting chariot. While this was taking place, Apollo rubbed an ointment onto Phaethon's face to protect him from the terrible heat of the chariot. Then, placing the bright diadem on the boy's head, he said, "Now, my son, listen to some last warnings if you can. These horses set their own pace. No need to urge them onward; the trouble is to hold them. Follow the wheel tracks. Do not go too high or you will set heaven on fire, and if you go too low, the earth will be scorched. Take the middle way; it is the easiest. For the rest, I pray that Fortune will take better care of you than you can of yourself."

Without bothering to answer, Phaethon, filled with the pride of his new power, sprang into the chariot, gathered up the reins and called a thanks to his father for the gift he had given so unwillingly.

PHAETHON DRIVES THE CHARIOT OF THE SUN

Apollo's horses sprang through the Gates of Dawn into the sky, swinging the chariot aloft behind them. Their swiftly galloping feet quickly lifted them through the low-lying sea mist. Soon the east wind was left far behind.

As they climbed the sky, all went well for a while. The way was steep, and as Apollo had said, the horses had difficulty making it. But when the course leveled off and the height of heaven had been reached, suddenly there was a change. The horses could feel that there was a lighter weight in the chariot than usual. A lighter hand held the reins. If their master was not driving, they were masters. As soon as they realized this, the horses left the path and began running madly, the chariot swinging wildly behind them from left to right.

Phaethon was filled with panic. He did not know which way to pull the reins to return to the path. He could not call to the horses because he did not know their names. He was powerless to control them. He looked below him once and sickened at the sight of the earth so far away. As it whirled beneath its vapors sometimes it showed the whiteness of its polar seas, sometimes its blue oceans came into view. But Phaethon was too frightened to appreciate the beauty of the compact globe beneath him. Once he looked back over his shoulder and saw that much of the sky lay behind him. But still greater vastnesses lay ahead. His knees shook, and he wished with all his heart he had never asked for this privilege. Even, he wished he had never learned the truth about his parentage. The taunts of his playmates were easier to endure than the terrible fear he was suffering now. What should he do?

In his despair a kind of numbness seized him, and the reins slipped from his hand. Immediately the horses seemed to go mad. They left the course completely and dashed about the sky wherever they wished. At last they climbed to the very height of heaven, then, plummeting down, they set the earth on fire. The mountains were the first to burn, then the meadows blackened. The flames devoured the

crops and, moving on, burned city walls and the luckless people within them. Everything was ablaze.

Phaethon, clinging now to the swaying chariot, was
surrounded with smoke and flame. The heat was a
torture, and he longed only to be dead.

Under the heat of the low-flying chariot, the seas
began to narrow. Where had been rolling water was
now dry sand. As the seas shrank, mountaintops which
had lain beneath the surface suddenly came into view
above the water, and islands appeared—the Cyclades,
which forever after dotted those seas.

At last Earth could bear no more. She felt the heat
of flames as her forests burned; she felt the waters of
her springs pulling deep within her to escape the fires
that would have consumed them. She knew that unless
help came fast, she was doomed. She cried aloud to
Zeus to save her, and the All-Father heard her cry.

Zeus summoned the gods, explaining to Apollo why
he must end the life of another son of his. And the
golden god stood with bowed head, not answering, for
he knew that he, too, was culpable. He had been an
unwise father in agreeing to grant any wish a young
boy might express. Now the earth had suffered from
that rash promise.

The first thing Zeus did was to throw a dense blan-
ket of fog around the earth. This smothered the flames
and put out the fires. Next he seized a thunderbolt,
and bracing himself carefully, he flung it at the racing
chariot. It struck like a bolt of lightning, splitting the

chariot in two and scattering the horses, who fled from the shattered ruin.

Phaethon, killed by the thunderbolt, fell from the chariot. His hair aflame, his garments burning, he arced through the sky, descending toward Earth in a trailing brightness such as a falling star gives to the night sky in autumn. In a faraway part of the world and a long way from home, the river Eridanus received his blackened body. But the nymphs of that stream raised it from the waters and buried it on the riverbank. Over the grave they placed a stone that bore these words:

> Here lies Phaethon, who tried to drive his father's chariot.
> He badly failed; but he had bravely dared.

APOLLO'S GRIEF

The golden god grieved so at the loss of this daring son that he let the world live in darkness for one whole day. No light showed anywhere except from the fires that flared again here and there with the passing of the fog. Clymene grieved, too, when the news of her loss reached her. Distracted, she wandered the earth until at last she found Phaethon's grave on the riverbank. She pressed the gravestone to her breast and watered it with her tears.

As for Apollo, he dressed himself in deepest mourning. No longer did he look a golden god. Rather it was as if the sun had suffered an eclipse. He even declared that never again would he drive the chariot of the sun across the sky.

"Let he who wants it have that task," declared Apollo. "I am tired of it. And if no one wants to take my place, then let Zeus try to control those horses. He will quickly see that failing to do so hardly merits death."

In his grief, Apollo began to resent his son's death. But the gods pleaded with him not to defy Zeus and not to shirk his duties as god of the sun. Even Zeus, moved by his son's terrible sorrow, apologized for hurling the thunderbolt, at the same time warning Apollo to choose his words with greater care when talking about the Lord of the Sky.

Then Zeus went carefully around the walls of high Olympus making sure that the fire had not damaged them. He found them in good condition. From the ramparts he looked down upon the earth, and when he saw it blackened and smoking, his heart grieved. Descending to Earth, he caused the springs to bubble up once more, and the streams began to flow. At his command the forests turned green again, and the meadows were covered with grass. Now it was up to man to build again on the earth what a willful lad had so nearly destroyed.

Orion

Orion was a mighty hunter and one of the handsomest men who ever stalked the earth. This was hardly surprising since he was a son of Poseidon. But even the god of the sea was impressed by the special qualities of this son, and so he bestowed upon Orion a privilege. Poseidon gave him the power of walking through water. It was a dubious gift.

Like Heracles, Orion wore a lionskin and carried a club. A heavy belt kept the lionskin in place around Orion's waist, whereas Heracles wore his flung over one shoulder.

Now it came about that Orion, always looking for new hunting grounds, learned that the island of Chios off the coast of Asia Minor was infested with all kinds of wild beasts. The king of Chios, Oenopion, had sent out word that he would give his daughter, Merope, in marriage to the man who could rid the kingdom of this danger. Less interested in Merope than in the chance for some good hunting, Orion happily set out for Chios. But when he arrived and beheld the fair princess, he fell madly in love with her.

Each day Orion went out into the fields and forests, and each night he returned home with the skins of the animals he had slain. He always presented these trophies to Merope in token of his love. Indeed this bloody tribute was his only means of telling her how dear she was to him.

The day came when the last wild animal was gone from Chios. Men could walk through the forests without fear, and no marauding creatures threatened the workers in the fields.

"Now, O king," said Orion, "I have earned the right to claim Merope for my bride."

But Oenopion put him off. And no matter how often Orion reminded the king of his bargain, it was always the same. At last the mighty hunter realized that Oenopion had no intention of living up to his promise and that Merope would never be his. Therefore he resolved upon a desperate course. He would take her by force!

So one night when all the palace was asleep, Orion crept into Merope's chamber and seized her as she slept. But when the princess felt his stout arms about her, she woke and struggled and screamed. That heap of hides and horns had not endeared her suitor to her, and she was no more eager to become Orion's bride than Oenopion was to give her to him.

Guards burst into her chamber, and Orion was overwhelmed. He was taken at once to Oenopion.

To everyone's surprise, the king seemed more amused than angered at the insult to his daughter. "Hot blood will boil over now and then," he told Orion. "You have long been tantalized by Merope's beauty. What you did is not surprising, though it was reckless and inconsiderate. Let us sit together now and share some wine and discuss this whole matter like reasonable men."

Orion who had expected a quick death when the guards seized him, was much heartened by these words. Perhaps the king was a just man after all and aware of his own responsibility in the misadventure. At the king's request, Orion seated himself, the wine was brought and poured, and while the guards stood at a discreet distance, the king and the mighty hunter talked.

As often happens, one goblet of wine led to another. The king poured with a generous hand, and before long Orion's head began to nod. The king watched him narrowly. Suddenly, Orion slumped forward onto the table, knocking over the goblet and spilling the last of the wine. He was in a drunken slumber. Instantly the king summoned the guard, and before Orion could waken, the king and the guards blinded him. The insult to Merope had been fearfully avenged. Next, Oenopion had Orion carried to the seashore and abandoned on the sands.

For hours he lay suffering and spent. Then there came up out of the sea a herd of seals. They lay down upon the strand to sun themselves. With them was their sealherd, Proteus, carrying his kelp-wreathed horn. When he saw the blinded man upon the beach, he comforted him with these words: "If you would have your sight restored, go to where the sun mounts the sky at dawn, and while you stare at it your eyes will see again."

"But how am I to find my way there?" asked Orion. "And how do I know that what you say is true? Who are you?"

"I am Proteus, the Old Man of the Sea, and I have the gift of prophecy."

Then Orion sprang eagerly to his feet. Surely Poseidon had sent this help to him! He would yet be saved.

"To find your way to the east, you must first find the forge of Hephaestus," Proteus told him. "Listen for the sound of his hammer and follow that sound. All will be well once you reach the forge."

Orion went to where the waves ran up the sand and stood listening. At last he heard the faint sound of a hammer coming to him over the waters. He took a step forward and another and another. Soon he was walking through the sea, in the direction of the sound.

It brought him to the island of Lemnos. Now the ringing of hammers was loud, and he had no difficulty locating the forge of Hephaestus. When the lame god saw how the mighty hunter had been crippled, he felt great pity for him.

"You shall have one of my boy workers to be your eyes," he told Orion.

A boy was chosen, and Orion lifted him to his shoulders. With the boy guiding him, he set out for the east. The way was long, but at last they came to where the sky and Earth meet at the Gates of Dawn. And when the chariot of the sun mounted the sky, Orion lifted his face to its warmth, and in a moment his sight was restored. Then, swinging his club fiercely as a portent of what he meant to do, he started back to Chios to take vengeance on Oenopion.

But the king eluded him. When news of Orion's approach reached the palace, Oenopion's subjects hid him in a deep cavern. And though Orion raged up and down the island, he never found him.

The mighty hunter then crossed the waters to the mainland and the province of Boeotia. One day when he was ranging the woods, he came upon seven beautiful nymphs dancing in a sunny glade. Holding hands, they danced in a circle, moving now to the right and

now to the left. These were the Pleiades, the daughters of Atlas. Orion was enchanted at the sight of them. But when he entered the glade to express his pleasure at their grace and loveliness, they fled before him. Orion gave pursuit, and so they raced down the forest aisles, the seven nymphs and the mighty hunter pursuing them. At last the Pleiades could run no farther, and they called on Zeus to save them. He quickly changed them into doves and placed them in the sky, where to this day we can see them.

Following this adventure, Orion journeyed to Crete. There Artemis was so struck by his good looks and his prowess as a hunter that she invited him to join the chase with her. She even gave him a dog, which he named Sirius. It went everywhere with him. Then, so handsome was he, Artemis began to think of marrying Orion. It is here that Apollo enters the story.

As soon as news reached him of what Artemis was considering, Apollo decided to take a hand in Orion's fortunes. It is not unknown for twin brothers to be jealous of their sisters' affections, and Apollo had no intention of letting Artemis wed Orion. So he played a cruel trick on her.

One day when the two were walking beside the sea, Apollo noted a small object far out upon the water. He knew it was Orion walking through the water with just his head above it.

"See that tiny spot out there on the ocean?" said Apollo to Artemis.

"Yes, I see it. What of it?" she asked.

"I'll wager that it is too small and distant a target for you to hit," returned her brother.

This was all the challenge the hunter goddess needed. She reached to draw an arrow from the quiver on her back. Quickly she fitted it to her silver bow, drew back the bowstring, and with a twang the arrow sped away. It found its target as Apollo knew it would, and before the day was gone, the body of Orion was washed ashore.

Weeping pitifully, Artemis placed Orion among the stars—his belt, his lionskin and his club. His dog, Sirius, she also placed with him.

And so even now the mighty hunter ranges the sky in the constellation which bears his name. And always before him flee the Pleiades.

Acteon

One day the young hunter Acteon, accompanied by his fifty hounds and a group of his friends, was led by the chase to the rim of a high cliff. Below them lay a small, heavily forested valley. It was noon.

"Comrades," said Acteon, "the sun god is halfway through his course, and our bags are full of game of every kind. Let us have done with hunting for the present and rest ourselves above this quiet valley."

They stretched themselves thankfully upon the forest floor, while their dogs flopped panting around them. For a while they talked and laughed in friendly give-and-take, and then Acteon rose and started over the cliff edge, following a little trail down to the valley.

Now this valley with its thick stand of pine and cypress trees had long been sacred to Artemis. Deep within the valley was a heavily shaded grotto, fragrant with the scent of violets and filled with the music of a little stream that issued from under a rocky arch, spreading its crystal waters into a deep pool. Here Artemis and her attendants were fond of bathing.

Arriving at the pool after a good hunt, the goddess would hand her bow and arrows to one nymph, her robe to another, while a third bound up her hair. This done, Artemis would plunge into the cool water and her nymphs, disrobing, would follow. After refreshing themselves, the nymphs and their goddess would leave the pool to stretch themselves upon the grass while they enjoyed the murmur of the little stream.

It was this scene Acteon blundered on when, following the strange trail, he came to the secret grotto. The nymphs saw him first and sprang to their feet with horrified cries. Swiftly they gathered around Artemis to shield her from the stranger's amazed gaze. But the goddess was taller than her companions, and as she looked over their heads at the intruder a painful blush reddened her from feet to forehead. For just a moment the goddess felt a dreadful shame, then anger surged upon her. She was outraged that a man should see her naked. She reached for her bow and arrows, but they were lying too far up the bank. Then, stooping, she scooped up a handful of water and flung it into Acteon's face, saying as she did so, "Now try to tell anyone that you have seen Artemis naked. Just try!"

Even as Acteon raised a hand to brush the water

from his face, horns began to sprout from his forehead. His neck lengthened. In another moment he had turned into a stag. Startled, and hardly knowing what he did, Acteon bounded away, amazed at his own speed. He stopped at last to look upon his reflection in a quiet pool. What he saw was more than he could bear. Tears ran down his stag face, and though he tried to cry out, no sound came from him. Yet were his heart and mind what they had always been. He tried to decide what to do. He dreaded returning to the palace. Besides the humiliation of his change, who would know him as Acteon, grandson of Cadmus, founder of Thebes? Should he seek some corner of safety in the forest? The decision was made for him.

Suddenly there broke out to one side the baying of hounds and the shouts of the hunters. They were calling him by name. "Acteon, Acteon!" they cried. "Where are you? Your hounds have scented game!"

With horror he saw his own hounds come bursting through the underbrush and realized that *he* was their game! He was being hunted by his own hounds! He tried to call out to them. But now he was a stag and mute.

With a bound he was off again, his hounds fiercely pursuing. Through brush, between trees, over rocks and streams they flew. It seemed to Acteon that his heart would burst and every breath was a pain. But still the hounds drew nearer.

They arrived at last at the very end of the valley where the rock cliffs rose up, closing it in. The stag could go no farther. At bay, he turned and saw the hounds, his hounds, racing toward him, their yaps and howls an orchestra of death. One leaped for his throat, another for a foreleg, and by the time the hunters had run up, the stag was dead.

"Ah, if only Acteon could have seen this work of his hounds!" said one.

"And he can take full credit for them since he trained them himself," said another.

"I wonder where Acteon could have gone?" asked a third.

In time, Acteon's fate became known, as such things always do. And ever after when hunters were following an unknown trail, they moved cautiously and avoided any formation in the forest that might prove to be a grotto. Such places could be dangerous, especially when sacred to Artemis.

Clytie

We have seen that Apollo was luckless in his loves. Some, like Daphne, escaped him. Others, like Coronis, betrayed him. One there was, Marpessa, who refused him when Zeus gave her a choice between Idas, a mortal, and the golden god who had promised her immortality in exchange for her love. Marpessa quite sensibly chose her mortal lover on the ground that even though she were immortal, she would still grow old, and she was sure Apollo would abandon her when age lined her face. Thus did Idas win a beautiful and sensible wife.

Clytie was something different. She fell in love with Apollo. She could hardly be blamed for this. Apollo was the most shining and beautiful of all the gods, and he was universally adored. But when she made her love known to him, he spurned her.

"I see nothing to love in you," he declared cruelly. "As for your love, I cannot cherish a heart so freely given."

Now this, of course, should have shown Clytie how utterly hopeless her love was. If her pride had not prevented her from declaring herself in the first place, his perversity and bluntness should have stifled any feeling she ever had for him. But so great was her infatuation that she could not bring herself to the point of relinquishing hope that one day Apollo's heart would be touched by her constancy instead of merely bored by it. She became that most absurd of all human creatures, a lovelorn girl.

Each dawn she would go forth from her father's house and seat herself on the ground in the garden where she would have an uninterrupted view of Apollo as he drove the chariot of the sun across the sky. Looking toward the east, Clytie's heart would leap with the first appearance of the sun god and her eyes would follow him faithfully as he crossed the sky. Not until night, when the western ocean engulfed him, would she return to the house, eat a bite of supper, and go mournfully to bed.

Of course Apollo saw her sitting there, and his heart was filled with disgust. Moreover, he feared that some of his fellow Olympians might learn about the love-

sick girl and start teasing him. The whole silly affair was most unbecoming to the god and to the maiden and it must be stopped, he decided.

So one day when Clytie was sitting in the garden as usual, watching with longing eyes the progress of the sun across the sky, she felt a strange lightness all through her body. Was the sun god working some miracle in her? Had his cold heart melted at last? Clytie tried to get to her feet, but she was rooted to the ground. Then her body began slimming until she was no wider than a flower's stalk. Leaves grew where her arms had been. Her features disappeared and her face grew round with golden petals like the sun's rays rimming it. Clytie had become a sunflower!

We see her still along country roads and in country gardens, holding her face to the sun and slowly turning it to follow him across the sky.

GLOSSARY

Acteon   ac tē'on

Admetus   ad mē'tus

Aegean   ē gē'an

Alcestis   al ses'tis

Aphrodite   ăf rŏ dī'tē

Apollo   a pŏl'ō

Arcadia   ar kā'dĭ a

Arcadian   ar kā'di an

Artemis   ar'tĕ mĭs

Asclepius   as klē'pi us

Athena   a thē'na

Atlas   ăt'lăs

Atropos   ăt'rō pŏs

Boeotia   bē ō'shi a

Cadmus   kăd'mŭs

Castalian   cas tā'li an

Charon   kā'rŏn

Cheiron   kī'ron

Chios   kī'os

Clotho   klō'thō

Clymene   klĭm'e nē

Clytie   klĭ'ti ē

Corinth   kŏr'ĭnth

Coronis   ko rō'nĭs

Cyclades   sĭk'la dēz

Cyclopes   sī'klō pēz

Daphne   dăf'nē

Delos   dē'los

Delphi   dĕl'fī

Eros   ē'ros

Hades   hā'dēz

Hebe   hē'bē

Helios   hē'lĭ ŏs

Hephaestus   he fĕs'tŭs

Hera   hē'ra

Heracles   her'a klēz

Hermes   hŭr'mēz

Idas   ī′das
Io   ī′ō
Iolcus   ĭ ol′kus

Lachesis   lăk′e sĭs
Larrisa   la ris′a
Leto   lē′tō

Maia   mī′a
Manto   man′tō
Merope   mer′ō pē
Midas   mī′das
Marpessa   mar pes′a
Moerae   mē′rē

Niobe   nī′o be

Oenopion   ē nō′pi on
Olympus   ō lĭm′pŭs
Orion   ō rī′on

Pan   păn
Parnassus   par năs′ŭs

Pelias   pē′lĭ ăs
Phaethon   fā′ē thōn
Pherae   fē′rē
Phrygia   frĭj′ĭ a
Pieria   pī ir′ĭ a
Pleiades   plē′a dēz
Pluto   plōō′tō
Poseidon   pō sī′dŏn
Proteus   prō′tūs

Silenus   sī lē′nŭs
Tantalus   tăn′ta lŭs
Tartarus   tar′tăr us
Thanatos   thăn′a tŏs
Thebes   thēbz
Themis   thē′mis
Thessaly   thĕs′a li
Thrace   thrās
Titan   tī′tăn
Tmolos   t mō′los

Zeus   zūs

ABOUT THE AUTHOR

DORIS GATES was born and grew up in California, not far from Carmel, where she now makes her home. She was for many years head of the Children's Department of the Fresno County Free Library in Fresno, California. Their new children's room, which was dedicated in 1969, is called the Doris Gates Room in her honor. It was at this library that she became well known as a storyteller, an activity she has continued through the years. The Greek myths—the fabulous tales of gods and heroes, of bravery and honor, of meanness and revenge—have always been among her favorite stories to tell.

After the publication of several of her books, Doris Gates gave up her library career to devote full time to writing books for children. Her many well-known books include *A Morgan for Melinda* and the Newbery Honor Book, *Blue Willow.*